DUCK in the TRUCK

For Gail

Duck in the Truck

Copyright © 1999 by Jez Alborough

Printed in Hong Kong. All rights reserved.

http://www.harperchildrens.com

First published in the United Kingdom by HarperCollins Publishers Ltd., 1999

1 2 3 4 5 6 7 8 9 10

First U.S. edition, HarperCollins Publishers Inc., 2000

ISBN 0-06-028685-7   37,933

Library of Congress Catalog Card Number 99-60934

DUCK in the TRUCK

Jez Alborough

HARPERCOLLINSPUBLISHERS

This is the Duck driving home in a truck.

This is the track which is taking him back.

This is the rock struck by the truck   and this is

the muck   where the truck becomes stuck.

These are the feet that
jump the Duck down

into the muck
all yucky and brown.

This is the frog who watched from the bush

and croaks, "I'll help you give it a push!"

This is the push of a Frog   and a Duck...

And this is the truck still stuck.

This is a sheep
driving home in a jeep.

"Get out of the way,"
he yells with a beep.

This is the quack of an angry Duck.
"I can't," he snaps, "my truck is stuck."

This is the quiet…

as they think
what to do.

"Got it!" croaks Frog,
"Sheep can push too."

This is the slurp   and squelch   and suck

as the Sheep steps slowly through the muck.

This is the push of a Sheep, a Frog   and a Duck

and this is the truck…   still stuck.

This is the happy sleepy goat relaxing on his motorboat.

This is the ear that hears the shout,

"My truck's in the muck and it won't come out!"

This is the rope
and here's the Goat's plan,

to tie a knot
as tight as they can.

This is the push at the rear once more

This is the pull of the boat leaving shore.

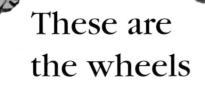

These are
the wheels

finally
gripping

TWANG

this is
the knot

suddenly
slipping

This is the truck with the wheels spinning fast

back on the track…   UNSTUCK AT LAST!

This is the Duck driving home in the truck

leaving the Frog, the Sheep and the Goat…

STUCK IN THE MUCK!